A COIN FOR ANDREW

DR. BARRETT K. HAYS

AuthorHouse™
1663 Liberty Drive
Bloomington, IN 47403
www.authorhouse.com
Phone: 1 (800) 839-8640

Published by AuthorHouse 09/25/2018

ISBN: 978-1-5462-6125-4 (sc)
ISBN: 978-1-5462-6126-1 (e)

Library of Congress Control Number: 2018911367

Interior Graphic Credit: Lowell Hilderbrandt

Print information available on the last page.

authorHOUSE®

A COIN FOR ANDREW

Titles to look for by this author:

Dr. Barrett K. Hays

Mars, Jimmy and Me • Mrs. Long and Herbert • Albert Yang • Riley and the Lion • A Book for Jesse • A New Dress for Hazel • Emile's Amazon Adventure Emile in London • Emile's Great Rescue

Author's Note:

A Coin for Andrew is dedicated to my roommate at Baylor University, Dr. Lee Au. The last time my wife Greta and I saw Lee, he and his lovely wife Dr. Sue Lynn Au had just had a new baby girl, Tiffany. So while Dr. Sue Au worked, the four of us drove around the island of Oahu and visited with his parents Drs. Francis and Cora Au.

Dr. Barrett K. Hays

Dr. Wang stood in the window of the small house on Mintor Street. His grandchildren were all coming over to celebrate his retirement. He had come far from home, but America had been good to him. He couldn't remember Shanghai or how it had looked so very long ago.

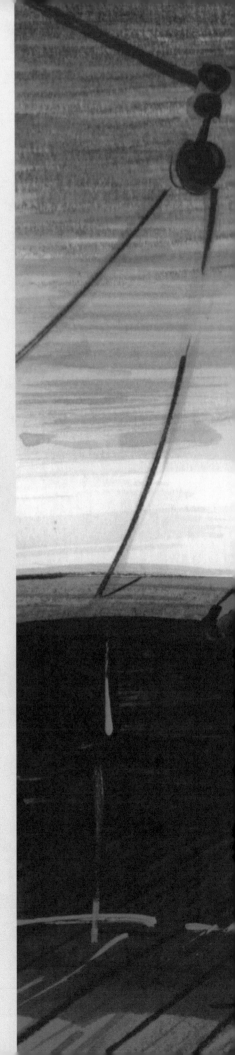

Dr. Barrett K. Hays

How he remembered the boat, and his parents waving goodbye. Some had spoken of war while others had spoken of peace. His father knew the winds of change were moving quickly through China.

In his father's time there had been wars with Japan. Japan had taken over Korea, and even Taiwan which China had controlled for centuries. Then there had been the Rebellion. His father had been involved in politics through a doctor who had trained in the U.S. It was him, the man his father had called Sun who convinced Dr. Wang's father to send him to the U.S. After all, until all China was unified there would be wars and more wars. Sun had asked his father to send him to a mission school in Hawaii. And perhaps after the wars which were surely coming, Dr. Wang could return to China, to home.

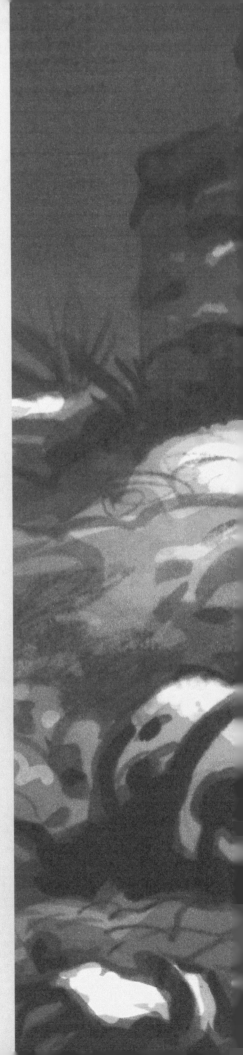

Dr. Wang's children began to arrive. How America had blessed them all. Henry, a successful CPA, and his wife Betty arrived with their children Susie and Tommy. They looked like children from Shanghai, but they didn't even speak the language. He usually spoke in Chinese at home, but with Susie and Tommy he was forced to speak English. He couldn't understand why Henry or Betty had never taught the children Chinese.

David had become a doctor, his wife Cora was a university professor. Their little baby Alexis was beginning to wake.

Then of course there was his son's son Andrew. Jeff Wang had been the smartest, the brightest boy in all the schools he had attended. He had been a superb athlete. Dr. Wang's smile turned to anguish as he again saw Jeff's identical twin in the form of his son walk up the drive.

"Grandfather, hello," he said in Chinese that was flawless. "My mother couldn't come because she had to work at the restaurant."

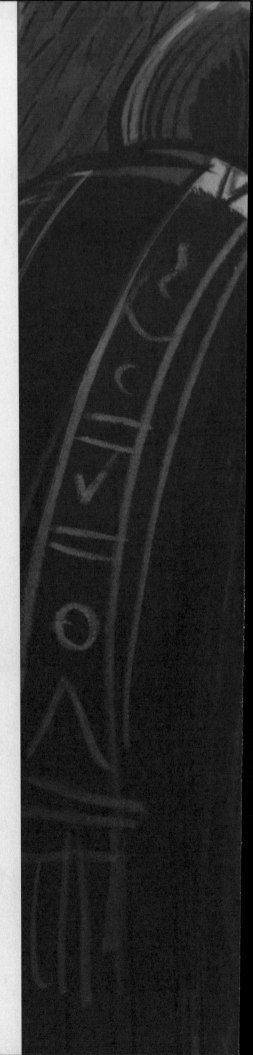

Dr. Wang had been against the marriage. However, the marriage took place. His son who had planned to be a doctor had married a girl who worked as a waitress in her family's restaurant. Poor girl had never been to college. The family had been horrified but true love had been stronger than the family. And the awful car accident which took Jeff's life had come so quickly, unexpectantly. And now here, his image, his essence still alive, moving on the earth.

"Grandfather, I'm so happy that you have retired. Now you can come to the restaurant and have lunch. Before, you have always been so busy."

"Maybe so, Jeff, I mean Andrew." Everyone was quiet as Dr. Wang entered the living room.

"When I came from Shanghai to the U.S., I was a very young man. I settled down and worked very hard so that my family and I could be proud of my accomplishments. I have been a doctor for forty-five years and I wish to do something different. Susie and Tommy here are envelopes for you."

"Grandfather, where is Shanghai?" Susie asked.

Dr. Wang seemed startled for a moment.

"Susie, Shanghai is a bustling seaport in China," Andrew said.

"Oh, Andrew is that where you learned to talk that funny talk?" stated Tommy.

"What's wrong with the way I talk? Both my Chinese and English are very good."

"Now children!" Dr. Wang said as he slipped one of the envelopes into his pocket.

The gift giving continued to all of the children and parents until Andrew was the last person.

"Andrew, and for you . . ." he said as he handed Andrew a sealed box.

Andrew opened the box and inside was an ordinary grayish old coin. "Thank you, Grandfather, I shall cherish your gift."

At last the gift giving was over, and everyone had left the living room.

"Grandfather, why did I not get money like all the rest?"

"I gave you the coin because it had been your father's. I have done all I can for the other children. The money, if used wisely, will come into good use for them. When you tell me everything there is to know about this coin, you and I will discuss it."

"Grandfather, I know nothing about coins."

"You will, and besides you and I will be having lunch tomorrow at the restaurant. I have some books about coins for you which I will bring with me."

"Oh, Grandfather," the little boy said as the biggest smile appeared across his face.

16

THE END

Printed in the United States
By Bookmasters